I0830741

WOUNDED WING

By
Richard Rashke

Illustrated
By
Julie Psenicka

WOUNDED WING

A Love Story for Children
Nine to Ninety-Nine

Copyright © 2026 by KR Associates

All rights reserved. No part of this publication may be reproduced, distributed, or transmitted in any form or by any means, including photocopying, recording, or other electronic or mechanical methods, without the prior written permission of the publisher, except in the case of brief quotations embodied in critical reviews and certain other noncommercial uses permitted by copyright law. For permission requests, write to the publisher, addressed "Attention: Permissions Coordinator," at the address below.

Published by KR Associates

Illustrations by Julie Psenicka

Book Cover Design & Interior Layout by Scribeworks, LLC.

Wounded Wing/ Richard Rashke—1st ed.

ISBN 979-8-9934698-5-0

For Paula

Prologue

Once upon
Long ago
In the ancient country of Japan
There lived a poor tenant farmer
Near Crystallake and
In the middle of a sweet smelling
Forest of pine
His name was Yohei

As the Game Warden
Of the Mighty Emperor
I came to know him well

His story is as pure
As falling snow
And I never tire of telling it
For it has changed
The way I look at life
And it will change you too
If you listen
With your heart

But I am getting ahead
Of myself

Yohei worked and worked for
His greedy landlord Jiro
Then he worked some more

Poor Yohei
After he paid Jiro rent of
Wild cherries and rice
Firewood and apples
Smoked Carp too
He was as poor as
When the year began

Life was hard and grim
And held no hope
Until

One Cold Winter's Morning

Part One

The Debt

CHAPTER ONE
The Gift

The sun is just beginning to peek over the horizon and paint the snow pink. The cold makes it squeak like a chipmunk when you walk on it.

I am a ball of feathers huddled in a clearing in the pine forest outside Yohei's hut. My alarm clock—the sun—awakens me. I pull my long beak from its warm bed under my feathered wing and stretch my slender legs to chase away the stiffness of the night. Dressed in pure white with splashes of black and red on my forehead, I dance a greeting to the new day.

The faster the sun rises, the faster I dance, sharing with the snow dusted pines all the joy I feel. I sing to the trees, as I do every winter morning.

> I am at home in the sky
> Born to soar
> To stretch my wings over wind
> > Fly Fly Fly
>
> Nothing to tie me to earth
> Born to fly
> To dance and glide through clouds or
> > Cry Cry Cry
>
> I am as free as light
> And all I can be
> Alone in the sky
> Just joy
> My wings and
> > Me
> > Me
> > Me

When the fireball sun creeps above the horizon, I peek through the window of Yohei's hut. I know it is a dangerous thing to do. Never leave the flock, we are taught. Outside of it, there is no protection. Stay away

from mortal men, we are taught. They cannot be trusted. But driven by curiosity, I break the rules of survival. You see, I am not like other cranes. I do not fit into their world because I am blessed with a special gift I received from my mother, who got it from her mother.

The first part of my gift is this: I can understand the words of mortal men, and I can pass this gift on to anyone I choose. I hope to give it to my own daughter one day, but I am in no hurry to have a crane baby. It is important that I carefully choose a husband because we cranes live for a thousand years. And when we bond, it is forever.

As I spy through the window, I see Yohei sleeping. Next to his futon, stretched out on the earthen floor, is a firepit ringed with fieldstones. The pit gives off the soft glow of night's sleepy embers. I watch Yohei stir, then sit up. With no one to say good morning to, he talks to his mother, long since dead from harsh winters and heavy work. I think the sound of his own voice makes him feel less lonely.

I quickly duck down from the window, press my back to the wall of the hut, and listen. I know I should flee, but I feel drawn to this mortal man. I do not understand why. Once again, I break the crane rules and do not fly away.

And So, My Story Begins

CHAPTER TWO

Trouble

I hear Yohei's gentle tenor voice:

> Mother
> I swear
> I heard a woman sing
> A voice as soft as flakes of snow
>
> But
> How can it be
> A woman here
> In a lonely forest of pine
> With wolves and wild boar
>
> Surely
> It is the wind
> Yes Mother
> Just a whispering
> Wind

I peek through the window again. Yohei is rolling up his futon. He slides open a paper screen and sets his bedroll on the bare ground of a storage room.

> But Mother
> Yohei says
> I swear I heard a woman
> Sing

I smile in delight.

A kettle filled with melted snow hangs over the firepit. Next to it sits a clay rice bowl and an empty clay cup. A simple vase of dried wildflowers perches on a wooden board fixed to the wall. The only things of value in Yohei's nearly bare hut are a large spinning wheel and a loom. Other than memories of love, they are the only things his mother left him when she died.

I watch Yohei sip a cup of sweet wildflower tea, and I listen to every aching word he speaks:

> Mother
> All I have is a ragged coat
> Holes in my pants
> A threadbare shirt
> Who will see me
>
> Mother
> All I have is a tiny hut
> Deep in the woods
> Where no one walks
> Who will hear me
>
> Mother
> All I have is an open heart
> And eyes with tears
> Waiting to cry
> Who will love me
>
> I sit near the fire
> When the moon is high
> While couples kiss and
> Touch and sigh
>
> Love smiles on them
> But passes me
> By

Suddenly, I hear tramping in the forest. It is Yohei's greedy landlord Jiro and his greedy wife Kane. They are trying to be as quiet as snowbunnies, but my crane ears hear every crunch of snow. To me, they sound like moose on their way to Crystallake. I do not like Jiro or Kane. The way they treat Yohei makes me angry. And I certainly do not trust them.

I quickly flee back into the forest. Hiding behind my favorite ancient pine tree with arching arms, I watch Jiro and Kane enter the clearing outside Yohei's hut.

I Expect Trouble

CHAPTER THREE

Gotcha

Wearing white winter hunting clothes, Jiro looks like a roly-poly snowman. He carries a bow and a quiver of arrows.

His wife Kane, dressed in quilted finery and fleece-lined boots, tags after him like a fawn. Her whisper thunders in my ear:

> Be careful my husband
> Don't get caught
>
> Get caught
> Jiro whispers back
> Who's going to see me in
> This forgotten forest
>
> Yohei
> Might see you
> Kane says
>
> Don't worry about
> That stupid farmer
> We own him
> Down to the torn rags he
> Wears

Kane begins talking to the trees with the pride of a blind wife. She says:

> Jiro is a hunter brave
> Fears nothing in the wild
> Bears
> Wolves
> Boars
> Whatever howls or roars
> Crane stew and a feather
> Bed

I watch Jiro creep forward, bent in a hunter's crouch.

He whispers:

> With only one arrow sharp
> As sly as a fox
> As quiet as a quail
> I'll kill the
> Bird I stalk
> Crane stew and a feather
> > Bed

As I quiver in fear, a shrill *kar-r-rooo* escapes from my throat, a warning to my brothers and sisters. I know I am in trouble as soon as I hear it shatter the morning stillness. Jiro stops, looks at Kane, then puts his finger to his lips.

> Sh-h-h-h
> He says
> I hear a
> > Crane

Jiro begins to pick his way through the pines like a hunter stalking a white-tailed doe, sly as a fox, quiet as a quail. It is too late for me to fly away, so I flee deeper into the woods. We cranes are swift and graceful when we wing, but slow and awkward when we walk.

Jiro sees me slipping between the pines. He looks around to make sure no one is following him, then draws an arrow from his quiver. I can smell his excitement. He lets the arrow fly. I scream *kar-r-rooo* as it pierces my right wing. It feels like the teeth of a fox tearing into my feathers.

Jiro hears my cry. He stands tall and says:

> Gotcha
> Gotcha

As Jiro waddles through the snow to the spot where I was standing, I move deeper into the forest. I jump in the air as if to take flight, then flap my good wing. I am able to coast forty feet before I hit the ground. I want to leave no trail of craneprints for Jiro to follow. I hear him say:

> Where did she go
> I know I hit her
>
> Here crane
> Here little crane

Jiro won't hurt you
Jiro likes pretty cranes

All he wants is
His arrow
                Back

If I were not in so much pain, I would have to laugh. Does that stupid mortal man think I would believe him? And at four feet tall, I am not exactly little. Ask a chickadee.

Okay, okay
Jiro says
Go ahead and hide
I don't care
Just last week
I shot two of
                Your Sisters

Yum
Yummy

And there's always a
                Tomorrow

Just as Yohei rushes out of his hut, Jiro turns and disappears through the pines with Kane trailing after him like a fawn. Yohei is dressed in torn pants, a winter hat of thatched straw, and boots of woven straw.

Since no one ever comes to visit Yohei except Jiro and Kane— and then only to demand more woodlogs or apples or smoked carp— Yohei calls out:

Esteemed Landlord Jiro
Is That Thee

CHAPTER FOUR
The Broken Arrow

When no one answers, Yohei mumbles to himself:

> More voices
> Before long, Yohei
> You'll hear cranes
> Talking

I watch Yohei untie a silk pouch filled with wild rice, as he does every winter morning. During the summer, he harvests the delicacy from the marshes that hug the shores of the Crystallake at the edge of the forest. He is supposed to give all the wild rice he picks to Jiro, but he always hides some for us cranes. We are the only friends he has. I often see him sitting at his window, watching us peck at the black specs scattered on the snow.

I am so scared, and in such pain, that the woods begin to spin. I know what I have to do, but I keep hearing my mother's voice in my head:

> Daughter
> Never Trust a Mortal Man

Wounded and unable to fly, I have no choice. Either I take a risk or die among the pines

> Alone

From my hiding place behind my favorite tree, I watch Yohei scatter the rice. I have always felt sorry for him. Every winter, I fly with my brothers and sisters away from the bitter cold of Siberia to the milder weather of Japan. As I fly, I think about the lonely farmer in the pine-scented forest near the marshes by the Crystallake. Could my wise mother be wrong? Are there mortal men a crane can trust?

I drag myself into the clearing. Whenever my drooping wounded wing touches the ground, a sharp pain flows through me like a river of lava. I bite back a cry. Yohei has his back to me, and he does not hear me crossing the snow. I collapse in a heap on my good wing and whimper softly.

Then I cry in fear and desperation:

> *kar-r-rooo*
> *kar-r-rooo*

Yohei spins around. Then he sees the ugly arrow poking through my wing:

> Oh, you poor thing
> Poor beautiful
> > Crane

He strokes my neck with fingers as rough as a pinecone, as soft as dew. I calm a little, but I am still quaking like a cornered snowbunnie.

> Do not be afraid
> Yohei says

His voice is soothing, and I pray to the crane gods that this mortal man can be trusted. I need him. I cannot fly with an arrow in my wounded wing. A hungry hawk is sure to find me. I *rooo* again. This time, my fear is wrapped in hope.

Yohei examines my wound and says:

> Do not cry
> Beautiful one
> Yohei is here
>
> You will soon
> Fly again
> Wings over wind
> But first
> The arrow
> > Be Brave

I plead with him, even though he cannot understand a word I say:

> Quickly
> Kind sir
> Quickly

Yohei snaps the arrow in two. Then, as swiftly as a magician pulls a rabbit from a hat, he slides it from my wing and tucks the pieces in the rope that is his belt.

There
He says
All done

Thank you
Kind sir
I say

Come inside
Yohei says
Before a hungry wolf
Finds you with a
Wounded wing

Yes, I say
But
Just until I can
Stretch my wings and
Fly Fly Fly

Yohei picks me up and carries me into his hut. Snuggled in his strong arms, a bundle of silk and feathers, I feel safe. I know I should not

But I Do

CHAPTER FIVE

The Last Coin

Yohei gently lays me down on the earthen floor, warmed by the fire. He says—as if I can understand him:

> Are you hungry

The hut pulses with loneliness and longing as Yohei tends to me. He gives me an earthen dish of water and a clay bowl of wild rice. As he washes my wound, he talks to me like he talks to his mother:

> It isn't much
> He says
> > But
> It is all Yohei has
>
> The water and rice
> Will make you strong so
> You can stretch your
> Wings over wind and
> > Fly

I am deeply touched. I know that he will not turn me into stew and a feather bed like a crane hunter with an arrow sharp.

Yohei prepares a warm place for me by the glowing embers. Then he removes the wildflowers from the clay vase and fishes out a piece of cloth with a single coin sleeping inside. He says:

> I have to leave you now
> But

I am sure he can hear the fear pounding beneath my feathers.

> But don't worry
> You'll be safe here in
> My humble hut

> Please don't go
> I beg
> If the hunter finds
>   Me

Yohei stares at the coin in the palm of his hand and says:

> This is my last coin
> I gladly spend
> It on
>   You

> But kind Sir
> I say
> I have nothing
> To give in
>   Return

Yohei walks out the door and heads for the village store. A few minutes later, Jiro and Kane storm into the clearing from different directions.

> Did you find her
> Kane asks

> No
> Did you
> Jiro asks

> If you wounded her like
> You claim
> Kane says
> She can't be far
>   Away

At the sound of their voices, I cover myself with my good wing to hide and listen.

> Don't just stand there
> Kane says
> Go finish her off

> Easier said than done
> Jiro says

> This crane is a
> Sneaky one
>
> Then be careful
> My husband
> If the Game Warden
> Catches you with a crane
> Dead or alive—
>
> Don't worry, my wife
> He never travels
> This far
>   North

As Jiro and Kane disappear into the forest to find and kill me, I peek out the window and *rooo* softly. What if they manage to find my tracks and follow them here?

I am so happy when Yohei returns before the hunter finds me that I fling open the door and greet him with a happy *kar-r-o-o-o*. He carries me to the nest he has made for me—soft cloth over straw mixed with crane feathers he harvested from the clearing. It was a kind thing to do, but the scent of the feathers makes me homesick for my mother and my brothers and my sisters. And the sky whispers to me like a lonely lover.

Yohei spreads the salve he bought with his last coin on my wounded wing. His touch is as soft as a mother's kiss.

The next day, I venture outside the hut for the first time. I am not afraid because Yohei stays by my side, as I limp through the fresh snow. He coaches me like a father crane teaching his daughter to fly. He laughs when I stumble.

> Not so fast
> He says
> Slow down
> Be careful
> Don't fall

The fluffy snow feels reassuring under my feet. The sting of winter cheers me. And the sun watches me from its perch in the sky with a curious eye. I feel happy. But the feeling confuses me. I am wounded. I am alone. I am a prisoner of pain. I am at the mercy of a mortal man I was told to fear.

> Why am I happy

I reason with myself:

You took a risk and trusted this mortal man
Because you had no choice
But now, you do

I look at Yohei wearing a worried frown.

I choose to trust

Now, every morning and afternoon, I exercise in the clearing. And every night, Yohei salves my wound. Slowly, my pain becomes a dull ache. With each flex of my mending wing, I feel stronger.

Early one morning, when I am nearly healed, a visitor walks into the clearing outside my nest. I hear him coming long before he arrives, and I rush to the window to see who it is.

Did Jiro learn that Yohei had bought salve in the village
Did he guess what it was for
Is he coming back

To Kill Me

CHAPTER SIX

The Visitor

Like a ghost from the netherworld, the Game Warden of the Mighty Emperor steps out of the pine forest into the clearing where Yohei is splitting wood with his sharp silver ax. He is a big man, tall and muscled, and frightening to a crane.

His boot prints in the snow are twice as large as Yohei's. He wears the leather of a samurai warrior. His jewel-handled sword is asleep in the scabbard at his side. He announces with imperial authority:

> I am the royal Game Warden
> I am looking for the
> Farmer they call
> Yohei

Yohei bows deeply. He is so shocked that he can barely speak.

> It is
> It is
> A-a-an
> Honor, Sir
> To-to have the
> Honorable
> Game Warden of the
> Mighty Emperor
> Visit a farmer as
> Worthless as this
> Man

The Game Warden grunts his approval, then growls:

> This is no
> Friendly visit
> Farmer
> I have come to command

> Your help
> In the name of the
> Emperor

Yohei bows deeply again and says:

> This poor peasant
> Doubts he can help a
> Warrior as important as
> Thee

The Game Warden grunts his approval.

> The villagers tell me
> You know this forest
> Like the inside
> Of your worthless hut
>
> You know the river rapids
> Its deep bends
> You know the rippling
> Green marshes
> And
> Each hidden cove on the
> Crystallake

Eyes downcast, Yohei bows again.

> Sir
> A little knowledge is all
> This servant has to offer
> Thee

The Game Warden again grunts his approval.

> The villagers tell me
> A hunter is killing
> Royal Cranes
> I'm here to find
> And
> Punish him
> I demand to know
> What you
> Know

Yohei bows even deeper.

Sir
What they say is true
Just last week
This foolish farmer
Found
A crane with an arrow
Through her
Wing

The Game Warden arches his eyebrows, grabs the hilt of his sword, and says in his most threatening samurai voice:

You're lucky I
Didn't find you
With a
Wounded Crane

I cringe in the hut with my ear to the door. No longer able to swallow my fear, I let out another *kar-r-rooo*.

Farmer
The Game Warden says
Did you hear that
It sounded like the
Cry of a
Bird

I peek out the window and see Yohei's face turn as white as the snow covering his straw boots. Will he lie to save himself? Or will he be as crafty as a falcon on the hunt? Yohei pauses, then says:

Sir
Thou art standing
In the middle of
A forest of snowy pines

Even in the darkest winter
There are many birds who
Cry and sing
It was probably a crane
Hiding and afraid
They come to
Eat the wild rice this
Poor farmer feeds
Them

In spite of my fear, I have to smile. Yohei did not tell a lie. But he didn't tell the whole truth.

The Game Warden tilts his head to listen. When he doesn't hear another *kar-r-rooo*, he draws himself up as straight as a spear, clears his throat, and thunders:

> The Mighty Emperor
> Has ordered me to deliver a
> Message to all his subjects
> Far and wide
> His message is this
>
> I, the Emperor, have decreed
> That no man has the right
> To hunt a royal crane
> To shoot it day or night
>
> I, the Emperor, have decreed
> That death shall befall
> The man who dares to kill
> What brings joy to all
>
> Every subject now must heed
> What I
> The Emperor has
> Decreed

Pleased with the Emperor's edict, Yohei promises to help the Game Warden. He says:

> The Mighty Emperor is just
> And this
> His humble subject
> Will gladly be his eyes and
> Ears

The Game Warden grunts his approval and turns to leave. Then he stops in his snow tracks and cocks his head like a robin listening for a worm moving under the grass. I am so afraid for Yohei, who is risking his life to protect me, that I let another rooo slip out of me like a burst of air.

The Game Warden glowers at Yohei with arched eyebrows and says:

> Again
> There it is again
> That crane
>
> It sounds like
> It's coming from
> Your hut
> What are you hiding
> There

Because Yohei cannot tell a lie, he says nothing. The Game Warden slowly unsheathes his sword. It gleams under the clear-eyed sun.

> Answer me stupid
> Farmer

At the sight of a sword as tall as me, I crawl into a corner of the hut. I tremble like a reed in the marsh hugging the Crystallake. I cannot stop myself:

Kar-r-rooo

CHAPTER SEVEN

Tsuu

The Game Warden bursts into the hut like the north wind. He sees me—a quivering ball of white, black, and red squeezed into a corner. He grunts in satisfaction and says to Yohei:

> Ah ha
> I thought so
> You're sneaky
> As a weasel
>
> What are you going to
> Do with her
> Make crane stew
> A feather bed
> Kneel

Yohei obeys and answers the only way he knows how. With downcast eyes, he tells the truth without a hint of fear. I beg the crane gods to guide and gild his tongue. Yohei says:

> Sir
> This foolish farmer
> Told Thee
> He found the crane
> With an arrow in
> Her wounded wing
>
> He brought her here to
> This bare hut so
> She can heal and
> Fly again
>
> I named her
> Tsuu

I like the sound of the name Yohei has given me. Tsu-u-u…Tsu-u-u. It sounds like the trill of a lark. I am pleased to have a name. We cranes do not use them. We know one another by the way we walk and smell, the timbre of our *kar-r-ooos.*

I knew from the moment the Game Warden spotted me cringing in the corner of Yohei's hut, he had made up his mind. In his most threatening voice, he says:

> A likely story, farmer
> Do you think I'm a fool
> Like you
>> Fool

The Game Warden raises his samurai sword, ready to strike. I do the only thing I can think of. I let out a fearsome scream from deep inside me. It is so fierce that I cannot recognize it as mine. The Game Warden is so startled that he lowers his sword. Yohei uses the pause to buy time. He says:

> Sir
> Please look around this
> Poor farmer's hut
> Thou wilt not find a bow
>> Or
> A quiver of arrows
>
> How can a farmer hunt and kill
>> Without
>> A bow and
>> Arrow

The Game Warden grunts his skepticism, sheathes his sword, and begins to search Yohei's hut. He finds the broken arrow next to the vase of wildflowers sitting on the shelf. He snarls:

> I thought so
> You're a
>> Trickster

Yohei makes one last effort to save his life. He says:

> Wise Sir
> How can a poor farmer hunt
> With only one
> Broken arrow and no
>> Bow

As the Game Warden hesitates, I rush over to Yohei and stand in front of him, a feather shield. I let out another fierce scream, ready to attack. Maybe, if I hit him just right with my strong wing, I can break his leg, then peck out his eyes with my pointed bill.

The sight of a Royal Crane prepared to die to protect a ragged farmer softens the Game Warden. He says:

> I see she's not
> Afraid of you
> Farmer
> She even seems to like you
>
> If she is willing to die for
> You
>
> I suppose you are
> Telling the
> Truth

The Game Warden lowers his sword.

> I'll be back
> Of that you can be sure
> And
> She better be
> Gone

Yohei lets out the breath he has been holding and bows deeply. The Game Warden storms out of the hut without bothering to close the door.

Yohei strokes my still shivering white feathers and says:

> You saved my life
> My beautiful
> Tsuu

When I hear Yohei call me his beautiful Tsuu, I feel a stab of something I cannot name. Even though I know he cannot understand me—oh how I wish he could—I say:

> I beg your forgiveness
> Brave mortal man
> Because of me
> The Game Warden
> Almost took your head

I promise
And to cranes
Promises are sacred
I promise I will find
A way to repay you

Someday Soon

CHAPTER EIGHT

Joy And Tears

The next morning, I wake early while Yohei is still asleep. He looks peaceful, as if he is having a sunny dream. As I watch him breathe, I see a smile at play on his face like a shy sunrise. Is he dreaming of me, his beautiful Tsuu? I bend over, embrace him with my wings and whisper:

> Goodbye
> Brave mortal man
> I must leave you now lest
> The Game Warden finds me
> Still here in your hut and
> And you die by his
> Sharp sword
>
> We will meet
> Before the
> Plum blossoms burst into
> Spring

I tiptoe out the door. Then I stop, turn around and look, for the last time, at the nest Yohei made for me of straw and feathers. I look at the lazy embers in the firepit. At his mother's loom. At the spinning wheel.

Then as Yohei begins to stir, I disappear into the forest of pine and hide behind my favorite tree. I hear him call:

> Tsuu
> Tsu-u-u-u

I watch him rush into the snowy clearing in panic. When he cannot find me, he looks up into the sky as if expecting to see me circling, wings over wind. He talks to me as he did inside our nest while I was healing. His words pierce my heart like pointed arrows.

> Goodbye
> My beautiful Tsuu

> May the strong winds
> Carry you
>
> May rays of sun
> Warm you
>
> May the marsh rice
> Feed you
>
> Come back again my, Tsuu
> When the snow hugs the firs and
> Paints their needles white
> Yohei will be
> Waiting

I flex my wings, then rise into the cold, clear sky, slowly at first, enjoying the smooth rhythm of my wings. A dancer above the earth. Weightless and free. I circle the clearing and what was my nest. Ribbons of smoke curl up from the opening in the roof. They reach up to tug me back.

I watch Yohei kneeling in the snow, his head on his chest. I am sure he is crying tears that are turning to ice under winter's breath.

I, too, weep. Oh yes, cranes cry, but not like mortal men. Our tears do not roll down our cheeks. They drip inside. On our hearts.

> Only now do I know that it is possible to be happy
> And To Be Sad

CHAPTER NINE

Can I Love Him

It is nighttime in the clearing outside Yohei's hut. The moon winks through scattered clouds and turns the fresh snow gold. I stand behind my favorite tree, staring at the hut. Embers from the firepit watch me through the window.

I have never been so afraid

Our crane code demands that I repay Yohei for saving my life. My mother and I had long chats about how I should do so. When I finally came up with a plan to pay the debt, she embraced it as if it were her own. She was wise. She saw what I could not see. She tells me:

> Do not be afraid
> My daughter
> Mortal men have
> Short lives
> They do not live a thousand
> Years

I do not find the thought reassuring. I inhale the night, hoping it will give me courage. Then I call on the second half of my gift and step into the clearing.

I am dressed in simple padded clothes. I wear boots of woven straw. My long black hair is a single braid, laced with ribbons of red, white, and black. I have delicate hands and feet. Straight white teeth. A shy smile. I have black eyes that glow and dance and cry.

I tiptoe to the window and peek in. Yohei is preparing his evening meal of bitter tea, rice, dried apples, and smoked carp from the Crystallake. My heart fills with aching memories of his nest that he called a hut. As I watch him, sad and alone, I argue with myself:

> He is so kind.
> He mourns each dying leaf fluttering to the forest floor
> I like him but can
> I love him

I turn and quickly walk back to the edge of the forest. It is not too late to go home. The choice is mine. I hesitate.

> He is so good.
> He smiles at every flower hiding in the shady woods
> Yes, I truly like him. But can
> I love him

I turn around and tiptoe back to Yohei's door and raise my tiny fist. Then I hesitate and walk away again. I stop. I have one foot in the forest and one foot in the clearing. Love, they say, is like a tiny seed.

> If the rain falls slow and the sun shines warm
> It will grow and
> Grow

I take another deep breath and welcome its icy sting. With my heart leaping against my chest, I timidly tap on the door.

> What if I cannot love him

It matters not, I say to myself. The debt must be paid. I rap louder. I know Yohei must be confused. No one comes to visit him except his greedy landlord. And he never comes at night when wolves roam in the dark.

Finally, Yohei calls out:

> Esteemed Landlord Jiro
> Is that
> Thee

Yohei eases the door open, then freezes like a raccoon caught stealing a hen.

> Who-who
> He stammers
> Can I
> Can I h-help you

> Yes sir
> I say
> Thank you
> I say

It is not a lie. My feelings are the blinding storm, and I am lost in confusion.

Come in
Yohei says
Warm yourself
You are welcome
Into my simple
    Hut

I step inside. I once felt safe and warm here as a crane. Will I feel
that way again as a woman?

Would you like a
Cup of hot tea
You must be as cold
As the waters of the
    Crystallake

Yes
Thank you
Kind sir

I see you are alone
Yohei says
It is dangerous for a
Woman as young
As you to travel
    Alone

Without telling a lie, I say:

It is not my habit to
Travel alone but
    Tonight

Tonight Is a Special Night

CHAPTER TEN

Maybe

Yohei pours hot wildflower tea. I hold the clay cup in my hands to warm them.

Visitor
Yohei says
Do not be upset
If
I was surprised by
Your nightknock on
My door

The only one who
Ever walked this
Deep into the forest was
The
Emperor's Game
Warden

My heart begins to race at the mention of the Game Warden. Memories of fear, and relief, and pride wash over me like a wave on the Crystallake.

Yohei seems far away and sad. After a long moment of silence, he asks my name.

I have dreaded the question that I knew would come. I pray that he listens with his heart.

My name
Kind sir
Is Tsuu
I say

Tsu-u-u
Tsu-u-u
Yohci sings
His voice is silkysad

> I once had a friend named
> > Tsuu
> She left to go home to
> Her family
>
> Though I have never
> Seen you before
> I feel we
> Have met in a
> Lovely dream
> Long since
> > Dreamt

I appeal to his heart again. I say:

> Good sir
> It was no dream and
> I tremble to
> Say your name
>
> You know my name
> Yohei asks
> But how
>
> I live so deep
> In forest of pine
> > Even
>
> Villagers cannot find
> > Me
>
> Your name is Yohei
> I say
> I met you once
> Not long ago
> You were kind to me then as
> > Well
>
> You must be mistaken
> Yohei says
> My eyes would never forget
> A face as beautiful as
> > Yours
>
> Thank you, kind sir
> But it is only with the

Heart
That one can truly
See

I am not sure if Yohei understands what it means to see with the
heart. I pray that, one day soon, he will. He says:

> Well
> Even if I do not
> Remember you
> I am pleased you
> Rapped on my lonesome door
> Where do you come from
>
> The far north
> I say
>
> Do you have family
>
> Many brothers and sisters
> I say
>
> You favor your arm
> Did you hurt yourself in
> The fierce night
>
> I bear a scar
> A reminder of cruelty and
> Kindness too
> I say
>
> Where are you going
>
> To repay a brave man
> Who saved my life
>
> Well
> Yohei says
> You are welcome to
> Stay here in
> My humble hut
> Until you are rested and
> Ready to travel
> Again

Yohei slides open the screen to his storage room as he did every night I lived with him.

I argue. He is so gentle, he could not harm a hare hiding in a hollow log. But can I love him?

Yohei returns with the futon and unrolls it near the firepit, as he did every night I lived with him. He says:

> Rest by the
> Embers still warm
> Yohei will
> Watch over you

Yohei covers me with the worn blanket that still holds my smell. A wave of peace and contentment ripples down my spine. Before I drift into the eager arms of sleep, I hear him say:

> Mother
> She came like a ghost
> From a dream I once had
> Fresh as the blossoms of spring
> I feel so lucky
> I could sing

> Mother
> She came like a vision
> A hope I once had
> Giving my poor heart a chance
> I feel so lucky
> I could dance

> Does it matter
> Who she is
> Where she came
> From

I am so happy to hear Yohei struggle with the doubt I planted. He is beginning to see with his heart. Someday, maybe he will have the courage to accept me as I really am. His beautiful Tsuu, dressed in white, with splashes of black and red, and legs as thin as hickory sticks.

I stay with Yohei. Then I stay some more. With each snowfall, he falls deeper and deeper in love until one cold starlit sky, as embers glow like sapphires, he asks me to be his wife.

Love, they say, is like a tiny seed. If rain falls slow. If the sun shines warm. It will grow, grow, grow. Maybe, I tell myself:

Maybe I CAN Love

Part Two

The Promise

CHAPTER ELEVEN

Trapped

One morning, a few weeks after Yohei and I spoke the words that bound us together forever, Jiro and Kane storm into the clearing. Yohei is splitting wood. I am stacking the pieces on a cart with wobbly wooden wheels. When the cart is full, Yohei will yoke himself like an ox and drag it down a rutted forest path to Jiro and Kane's mansion on the shores of the Crystallake.

> Yohei
> Jiro shouts
>
> You thief
> Kane yells
> Why didn't you tell us
> You took a
> > Wife

I begin to tremble at the sight of this hunter who tried to kill me. I want to run and hide behind my favorite tree. But my husband's steady voice calms me.

> Welcome
> Yohei says
> This poor farmer never sees
> His esteemed landlords
> > Except
> When they are cold and
> > Hungry
>
> Cut the poor farmer talk
> Jiro says
> You owe us
>
> Now that you're married
> Kane says
> You have to pay more rent

Chop more wood
Jiro says
Harvest more rice

Pick more plums
Kane says
And more
            Apples

But how
My husband says
This poor man can
Barely pay you now and
This ax cannot cut
            Faster

You can't fool us
Fool
Kane says
You have
            Money Money

And you've been
Hiding it from us
Jiro says
You little sneak

But
My husband says
This miserable man is as
Poor as a
            Grasshopper

Of course you have money
Jiro says
You bought a
            Wife

But esteemed landlords
My husband says
I did not buy
            Tsuu

Jiro and Kane burst out laughing. I pray that the gods will make them choke on their poison words.

Did you hear that
Jiro says
He didn't buy the woman

You think we are
Idiots
Kane says
Who would marry a creature as
Low as you

You spent our money
Jiro says
On a wife just
To please yourself

How ungrateful
Kane says
How selfish

Be sure of this
Jiro says
You will pay it back

All the money
You owe us
Kane says
         Money Money

I feel Yohei's helplessness. Jiro and Kane are standing in the clearing they own. They are stamping their cold feet to keep warm. On land they own. Outside a hut they own. Next to a woodpile they own. But that is not enough. They want more.

How can mortal men be so cruel

I can do nothing but watch them prance around the clearing, jesting, mimicking, chanting. Jiro takes the lead. Kane follows.

Double hands
Cut more
Double arms
Chop more
Double the rent

Double backs
Bear more

        Double legs
        Push more
        Double the profit

        We double your trouble
        And double our take
        Because
        We are landlords
        And that's what
        Landlords Do

    Jiro and Kane skip back into the pine forest, giggling like children just let out of school.

        My Husband
        I say
        Do not despair

    Not All Is Lost

CHAPTER TWELVE

The Sacred Promise

But how can I pay double
My husband says
I do not know what to do
    If if
You want to leave me
    My wife
    My Tsuu
The pain will be like a
Piercing arrow winged from a
    Bow

I am deeply moved by his pain, his love for me.

I am your wife forever
I say
I will stay
I will help

But how
Your arms are as thin as the
Reeds in the
    Marsh

I am a good weaver
I say
On the loom
Your mother left you
I say
I will weave a
Beautiful cloth of silk to
    Sell

Can you
Can you
My husband says
Then

I can pay Jiro and Kane the
Money I do not owe and
We can stay together
Husband and wife
          Forever

Yes
I say
But first you must make me a
Promise

Whatever you ask
I promise

You must not open the
Sliding screen
I say
          Or
Look upon me as
I spin and
          Weave

I do not know why
You ask this of me
But yes
I promise not to
Look upon you as
You spin and
          Weave

Yohei carries his mother's loom through the sliding screen to his storage room. Then he carries in the spinning wheel. As he lies down by the hot embers to rest and wait, I enter the storage room and begin to spin thread. When I have enough, I sit at the loom and start to weave the cloth that will save us. The only sound is a soothing lullaby.

tara-tara-tara
tara-tara-tara

As the shuttle slides and the
Loom Rocks

When I finish the cloth, it is early morning. The sun has not even winked its weary eye over the horizon. Yohei is still asleep. I stroke his brow until he wakes. Then I give him the cloth I have woven. It is

shimmering white, tinged with pink.

Yohei presses the cloth to his cheek. He is so relieved and happy that I feel proud I could help him. He says:

> I have
> Never caressed cloth so
> Soft so silky
> It will fetch
> A pleasing price
>
> You have worked hard
> My wife and
> Are tired
>   Rest

My husband eases me down on the futon, still cozy with his warmth. He covers me with the old worn blanket just as Jiro and Kane enter the clearing.

> Yohei
> They shout
> Oh Yo-o-o-hei
>
> Be careful
> My husband
> I warn
>
> I will
> He says
> Jiro and Kane were born
> With hearts as
> Hard as ice and just as
>   Cold
>
> Yohei
> O-o-oh
> Yohei, Jiro calls
>
> Time to pay what you owe
> Jiro shouts
>
> You can't hide from us
> Kane Calls

Yohei picks up the cloth I have woven and walks through the door to greet them. As exhausted as I am after working all night, I rise from the futon and

Watch From the Window

CHAPTER THIRTEEN

The Smell of Greed

Pay up, Jiro says
Or pack your rags

And get out
Kane says

I will pay what I
Do not owe
My husband says
    See

Jiro and Kane finger the silk cloth I wove. Their greed smells like summer sweat. Kane says:

Oh my
Oh my
As soft and pink as a
    Sunset
It will make a kimono
Fit for the
    Empress

As soon as this
Poor farmer sells it
My husband says
He will pay what
Thou say he owes

You
Kane says laughing
Sell
To the Empress
What do you know about
    Selling

The samurai will stop you
At the Mighty Emperor's gate

Jiro says
You're just a farmer with a
            Ragged coat
Holes in your pants and a
            Threadbare shirt

Let me-e-e sell the cloth
Kane purrs
I have a keen ear for the
Clink of a
            Coin

I want to shout:

            My husband!
      Do not listen to them
        Do not trust them
    You cannot bargain with greed
          It has no ears
    Its heart is withered by hunger
            It is blind
        But I know that you
            My husband
    Are smarter than those two fools
I know you will do what is best for our love

Jiro says:

            Kane will make sure
            You don't get cheated
            We'll take out what
            You owe

Kane says:

            Then give the rest to
                  You

My husband wavers.

            Maybe
            My esteemed landlords
            Are right
            This ignorant farmer knows
            Nothing of
                  Selling

I watch my husband give the cloth I wove to Kane. My human body aches. My craneheart is sad and heavy. I look on as Jiro and Kane prance around the clearing like two court jesters.

> To the royal court I go
> Kane chants
>
> To the royal court she goes
> Jiro chants
> With a pretty cloth to sell
>
> With money to be made
> Kane chants
> Before the thing can fade
>
> To the royal court she goes
> Jiro chants
> With soft silk to
> Sell

Jiro and Kane disappear into the pine forest. Their peels of laughter are a slap in my face. The last words I hear are:

> To the Royal Court we go
> Money Money

CHAPTER FOURTEEN

Gold

Two days later, I am brewing morning tea when I hear Jiro and Kane tramping through the pine trees. I creep to the window to watch. I am as quiet as a thought. They enter the clearing and kneel in the snow.

> Show me again
> Kane says

Jiro digs a shallow hole in the snow. Then he pulls a leather pouch from his pocket and pours a stream of gold coins into the hole. Kane runs her fingers through the coins. She says:

> Life is so sweet
> It tastes like honey
> When you have
> Money money
> Lots of money
>
> Life is so bright
> Jiro says
> Every day is sunny
> When you have
> Money money
> Lots of money
>
> Money makes you pretty
>
> Money makes you tall
>
> With money
> Kane says
> Lots and lots of money
> You never have to crawl
>
> Life is a ball
> Jiro says
> Every day is sweet as honey
> When you have
> > Money money

Lots and lots and lots of
Money

When Jiro sees Yohei walking out the door to greet them, he
scoops up all the coins but one. Then he drops them back into his leather
pouch and quickly stuffs it back into his pocket. He says:

Yohei
Today is your lucky day

My esteemed landlords
Got a good price

Not nearly as much
As we had hoped

Kane says
But
Enough to pay
What you owe
US

Jiro gives my husband the single coin.

Gold
My husband says
I have never had a
Coin of gold
My wife will be pleased
We thank
Thee

We are glad we
Can help a
Poor farmer get ahead
Kane says

Order your wife to
Weave another cloth of silk
Jiro says

To take to the
Mighty Emperor Himself
Kane says
For a new kimono

70

Kane will sell it
Jiro says
For a small commission
          Of Course

I don't know
My husband says
My poor wife worked
All night
            To
Weave the cloth
Thou sold
She needs rest

Suit yourself
Jiro shrugs

Go ahead
Kane shrugs
Give up the chance
To buy what you
            Need

A sharp new ax
Jiro says
A new fishing net

A pearl comb for
Your wife's pretty hair
Kane says

This poor farmer
My husband says
Does not know
What To
            Do

Just one more
Jiro says
Then she can rest

Well
My husband says
This simple woodsplitter
Thinks his wife is

Strong enough to
Weave one
          More

Of course she is
Kane says
We women are stronger
Than men will ever
          Admit

All right
My husband finally says
But Just
          One More

We always knew
You were a wise man
Jiro says
Who understands
The ways of the
          World

And a good husband who
Provides well
Kane says
And a husband soon to be
          Rich

I see Kane suppress a smile. My sensitive crane ears hear her whisper to Jiro:

Not if we can help it

Before my husband comes inside, I crawl back on the futon and pretend to be asleep. I know he does not want me to watch Jiro and Kane lie, cheat, and make a fool of him. I know he is afraid that his shame will make me think less of him as a mortal man.

My husband gently shakes my shoulder, shows me the coin, and says:

See what you earned
          Gold
If you could weave
Another cloth
We would have enough to

Live on for more
Than a
Year

Yohei's eyes plead with me, and I cannot refuse. I know that Jiro and Kane will cheat him again. But I cannot bring myself to dash his hopes. Although I do not understand the ways of mortal men, I am certain their greed will be our revenge someday. I say:

But this must be
The last

I promise
My husband says

I am so tired and sore that I sleep all day. That night, before I go to work in the storeroom where the spinning wheel and loom are awake and waiting, I say to my husband:

Remember
You cannot open the door
                Or
Look upon me as
I kneel behind
Your mother's spinning wheel and
Sit at her loom

I promise
My husband says
I will not look
But why I do not
                Understand

I slide the paper screen open and close it quietly as my husband lays down on the futon next to the dozing embers. The only sound in the quiet night is the soothing song of the loom.

Tara-tara
Tara-tara

CHAPTER FIFTEEN

Sleep My Love

It takes me much longer to make the second cloth. When I am finished, I ache, and my fingers are numb. I set the loom aside and step back into the hut. My husband is asleep. I watch him for a while, then I touch his shoulder. He wakes and I present the cloth.

My husband looks so pleased that it is worth all the tire and pain just to see him smile. He rubs the new cloth against his sleepy face.

> This one
> He says
> Is silkier and rosier
> Than the
> > Last

I am proud of my work, but I am so weak that I stumble. My husband catches me and helps me onto the futon that still smells of his love. He says:

> You look so tired
> My love
> > Sleep

As I close my eyes, and before I drift into the land of dreary dreams, I listen to Yohei sing a lullaby so tender that it brings tears to my eyes. So, this is what happens when mortals cry. Salty water. Wet and warm. On my cheeks.

> Close your eyes
> My love
> Rest your weary head
> May the moon above
> Send you warm dreams
> Sleep
> My love
> > Sleep

Breathe softly
My love
Rest your weary head
May the stars above
Send you sweet peace

When you awake
I will be here
For my love is forever
And yours to keep
Sleep
My love
Sleep

I wake up before the lazy sun. Yohei is breathing peace and does not stir. I stroke his cheek and plead from my craneheart:

You listen to the hidden lark
My love
Calling from a willow tree
You hear a burst of joyful noise
A gleeful melody

But stop and listen with your heart
My love
Take the time to see
He calls not only to his mate
He sings because he is free

You look at the cherry tree
My love
Warmed by dawn's creeping light
You see the buds of palest pink
Burst open
Grow bright

But stop and
Watch with your heart
My love
Take the time to see
She is spreading her petaled arms
To host the hungry bee

My husband
I beg you
See your Tsuu

With Your Heart

CHAPTER SIXTEEN

Just One More

Several days later, Jiro and Kane step into the clearing outside
our hut while we are resting after a morning splitting and stacking wood.
They wear expensive new clothes and boots. They call out sweetly:

> Yohei oh
> Yo-o-o-hei
>
> Today is your lucky day
> Jiro says
> Lucky
> Lucky man
>
> I sold the cloth to
> The Mighty Emperor Himself
> Kane says
> For twice as much
>
> Your share is double
> Jiro says

From the window I watch Jiro give Yohei two gold coins. He
hides his disappointment.

> This poor farmer thought
> Thought
> His wife will be very
> Pleased
>
> I will fetch even more
> For the next cloth
> Kane says
>
> There will not be
> A next cloth
> My husband says
> The weaver is worn
> And weary

And needs her
Rest

Another cloth
Jiro says
Will make you rich

Then your pretty wife
Kane says
Can sleep until the snow
Changes into water and
The cranes fly north

But this husband promised
        No More

Promised
Kane says
Did you hear that
Husbands always make
Promises they
Do not intend to
        Keep

Just one more
Jiro pleads
As a favor for your
Good friend Jiro

No
My husband says

Please
Kane pleads
You m-u-s-t help us
We spent all our
        Money
We are deep in debt

I bought a better bow
Jiro says
And a jeweled
        Sword

I bought a new kimono and
A long soft *Obi*

Woven with strands of
Silver and gold to
Wrap around
        My Waist

I bought a new horse
Jiro says
The best of course and
More land around the
        Crystallake

Isn't life grand
Kane says

But how can this
Poor peasant help
        You
My husband says
He is just an ignorant
        Farmer

True
Kane says
But he is married to a wife
        Who
Can make us all
        Rich

When my husband turns his back on Jiro and Kane, my body swells with pride. Yohei has stood up to his greedy landlords and kept his promise to me, that the second cloth would be the last.

You dare say no
Jiro shouts
Then we'll drive you out
Take back our hut

We'll find another stupid
Farmer to cut and
Split our wood
Pick our apples
Kane says
Harvest our wild rice
Smoke our carp

Thou cannot do that
My husband says
This worker with calloused
          Hands
Already paid the debt
          He did not
          Owe

So what
Jiro says

Who cares
Kane says

It is not fair
My husband says

Fair
Did you hear that Kane

Fair is for the rich
Kane says

All the poor get
Jiro says
Is more work

It makes this broken man
Very sad
My husband says

But
Thou leave him
          No Choice

He will beg his wife to
Weave one last
          Cloth

I feel sad too. Sad to see my husband cheated. Sad to see him humiliated. Sad to see him crushed like a grape. Then I hear Jiro and Kane deliver a final blow to a man who is already down.

Of course
Kane says
Just one last cloth

We wouldn't want your wife to
Get sick

Surely not
Jiro says
A sick wife can't
        Weave

    Jiro and Kane turn their backs on my husband. He stands in the clearing, shoulders sagging, head bowed. He walks to the door slowly as if he is afraid to come inside and

Face Me

CHAPTER SEVENTEEN

Your Day Will Come

My husband offers me the two gold coins and says:

> I know they are cheating me
> But I have no choice
> Jiro and Kane own me
>
> No, my husband
> They own your hut
> But not your
>> Home
>
> They own the fields and
> The trees you tend
> But not your
>> Hands
>
> They do not own
> Your generous heart
> Your brave soul
>
> And never never
> My husband
> Can they own
>> Our Love

Yohei holds me tight. His face is stained with tears, salty, wet, and warm. He whispers:

> My Tsuu
> I know I promised
>> But
> I must ask you to
> Weave one last cloth
>
> My husband
> I say
> I know you had no choice

I free you from the
Shackles of your word
I will weave the
        Cloth

My wife
I feel as helpless as a crane
        With a
Wounded Wing

I do not have a
Mound of gold
My husband says
        Or
Royal friends
        Or
A pointed spear

It is not fair
I do not despair
My day will
        Come

I believe in
The light of truth
In the might of right
In the power of love
Hate will not win the
        Fight

Without this hope
How can I face each
        Night

As sure as
A crane has wings
As winter smiles into spring
As the cherry trees burst pink
        My Day Will Come

And when it does, I want to be at his side, his cranewife, his
beautiful Tsuu.

Oh yes
I tell my husband

> Your day will come
> If not today
> Tomorrow then
> And bring an end
> To pain and
> > Sorrow

I go to his mother's waiting wheel to prepare the thread for my final cloth. It takes all the strength and courage I have. But I am determined to finish it.

After what seems like hours, I hear Yohei talking. I stop spinning to rest and listen.

> Mother
> He says
> She came like a ghost
> From a dream I once had
> Fresh as the blossoms of spring
> I feel so lucky
> I could sing
>
> Does it matter
> Mother
> Who she is or
> Where she is from
> Tsuu has won my heart
> Brought together never to part
> Lucky, lucky man
> > But
> Who Is This Tsuu Of Mine

When Yohei does not hear the wheel rock or the loom sing, he creeps to the paper screen. He says:

> My wife
> Are you all right
> Do you want water
> Some rice
> Tsuu
> Tsuu

Then my husband breaks his

> Sacred Promise

CHAPTER EIGHTEEN

Betrayal

I cannot describe the look of horror on my husband's face when he sees a crane kneeling beside the spinning wheel. She holds a white feather in her beak. Her chest is splattered with blood. A small pile of red-stained feathers sits on the floor next to her. I hear him gasp as he quickly slides the door closed.

If Jiro and Kane have left my husband no choice, Yohei too has left none for me. He has broken his promise. Betrayed my trust. Severed our bond. I have paid my debt. Now I am free to leave this nest I once loved, fly back home where I belong.

I flee out the back door, hide behind my favorite tree, and wait. For what and why, I do not know. Part of me wants to fly away, wings over wind. Part of me wants to stay. I am confused. But the crane world knows no confusion. We are born with instincts to guide us. We live in the flock to protect us. We are creatures of habit, duty, and honor. They bring certainty, pride, and security.

A few minutes later, I see Yohei rush out the door into the clearing. It is a moonless night, and I feel as dark as the sky above. I hear Yohei call:

> Tsuu
> Tsuu
> Come back
>
> I'm sorry
> Please come
> B-a-a-a-ck

I feel the pain and panic of his voice. But I cannot go back to him. I listen as he speaks through his tears. I can almost taste them, salty, warm, and wet. I hear him speak to himself:

> Yohei
> Tsuu asked you not to
> Look

                    You promised
                    What have you done

        Yohei calls to me:

                    Tsuu
                    I know you are there
                    What can I do to
                    Win you back
                    Please Tsuu
                    Please forgive
                              Me

    I stand as still as I do when I wait for a carp to swim by in the
waters of the Crystallake. And I listen as he speaks to his mother like a
wounded son.

                    Mother
                    When she looked at me
                    Eyes twinkling bright
                    The room began to glow
                    Why didn't I hold her tight
                              Why did I let her go

                    Mother
                    When she laughed with me
                    Eyes burning bright
                    My cares melted away
                    Like snow
                    Why didn't I hold her tight
                              Why did I let her go

                    You drove her away
                              Fool
                    No one to blame but you
                    Foolish foolish
                              Man

    I watch Yohei shuffle back to his hut like an old, tired farmer.
The moonless sky calls to me. I fly away. Wind under wings. With joy
and sorrow. A crane woman with

            Twohearts

Part Three

Redemption

CHAPTER NINETEEN

The Heart Speaks

Who am I
A crane or a mortal
Whose code do I follow
That of my flock or that of mortal men
If that of mortal men, what is expected of me
There is no map to guide you when you walk between
Two Worlds

The truth is, I know the answers, but I am afraid. My mother gave me the same advice I once gave the mortal man who was my husband and is no more.

My daughter, listen to your heart and you will know
And you will not fear

I convince myself it is my duty to return and watch over Yohei. What I would do if he was in danger, I do not know. I hide behind my favorite tree, waiting to see him come out to greet the day. To say a prayer. To sprinkle wild rice. But before Yohei leaves his hut, I hear Jiro and Kane walking through the pines. They are laughing and singing like children on a sled.

Life is a ball
Every day is sunny
When you got
Money
Money
Money

Yohei steps into the clearing to greet them. His hair is loose and uncombed. He walks as if he is carrying a pine log on his shoulders.

Go-o-o-d morning
Yohei
Jiro sings

Did your wife finish
Weaving her cloth
Kane asks

No

Why not
Kane says
You promised

She is gone

Well, don't just stand there
Jiro says
Go find her

This simple man does not
        Know
        Where she
        Is

She can't be far
Kane says
She's just a woman

Be quick about it
Jiro says
We need the cloth

We are up to my *Obi*
In debt

Ruined
Jiro says

    Yohei stands still, eyes cast down. What can he say? That he can't
find me because I flew away?
    Kane says:

If you won't go look
Lazy farmer
Then we will find her

And drag her back
By her long black hair
Jiro says

We will punish her with
A hickory switch
Kane says
To teach her how to obey

She can't do this to us
Jiro says
Who does she think
She is

Someone special
Yohei says
Someone this foolish man
              Lost

Yohei walks away, still bent like an old man carrying a log of pine.
I hear him mumble in a daze:

I have a wounded heart

And eyes with tears
Waiting to cry
With no one to love me

Foolish man
You held a moonbeam
In your hand
You let her
              Go

I want to run to him. To be his wife again. His beautiful Tsuu.
But I stay hidden behind my favorite tree and wait for night to seduce
him into the restless arms of sleep.

When the moon is high and the woods are windless, I creep to
the hut. I have long black hair. Tiny hands and feet. A shy smile. Black
eyes that smile, dance, and cry.

I peek in the window. Yohei is asleep. Exhausted by guilt and
sorrow. He looks as pale as fog hovering over the Crystallake. I ease the
door open. Tiptoe into the hut. Sit down beside him. I wonder what he
dreams. Is it about me? His beautiful Tsuu?

I think about his kindness when he carried me into his nest. A
bundle of bleeding feathers. I think about how he spent his last coin on
me. How he washed and salved my wounded wing. How he nursed me
like a papa crane. How he watched over me as I tried to walk in the snow.
But in spite of the warming thoughts, I cannot forget his broken promise

It hurts More Than the Hunter's Arrow

I speak softly to Yohei so as not to wake him. How can I ever trust you again, I ask? Then I stop and listen to my heart.

Can it be in the nature of mortal men to make mistakes, my heart asks
To use pain and loss to help them grow, my heart asks
Isn't it time to forgive, my heart asks

I bend over and brush Yohei's lips. I whisper:

Breathe softly
My love
Rest your weary head
May the stars above
Send you sweet peace
Sleep
My love
Sleep

Love they say
Is like a tiny seed
If the rain falls slow
And the sun shines warm
It will
Grow grow grow
But can I love him

Oh yes yes
I love this mortal so
And my love is forever
And his to keep
Sleep
My Love
Sleep

I lean over and kiss my husband again. Lips as soft as a plum blossom. Then I leave the hut. Dressed in white and black and red, I wrap myself in the icy cloak of night and wait for my alarm clock sun. For whatever surprises and sorrows the

Newborn Day Brings

CHAPTER TWENTY

As Sly as a fox

Yohei is splitting wood with angry blows, as if the log sitting on his chopping block is Jiro. Now and then he grunts like the Royal Game Warden of the Mighty Emperor. The broken arrow is tucked in his woven rope belt. A reminder of his beautiful Tsuu.

Yohei stops. He raises his head and looks up, expecting to see me circling in the brooding winter sky.

Jiro and Kane barge into the clearing shouting like angry parents. Jiro carries his new bow and quiver of arrows.

> Yohei
> Pack up your rags
> Jiro says
>
> Get out of our hut
> Kane says
>
> But
> Where will I
>   Go
> Yohei pleads
> What will this poor farmer
>   Do
> How will he
>   Eat
>
> Who cares
> Jiro says
>   Just

He spots the arrow in Yohei's belt.

> Where did you
> How did you
> Get my arrow

Is this your arrow
Yohei says
This foolish woodcutter
Found it
Esteemed Landlord

Well
I lost it, Jiro says
Give it to me

Yohei is such a good actor that even I believe he really does not know the arrow came from Jiro's quiver. Jiro yanks the arrow from Yohei's belt.

It's broken
He says
Look Kane
The idiot broke
My arrow

You owe us a
New one
Kane says
There must be something
We can take

The ax
Jiro says
The ax for the arrow a
Fair Trade

Jiro tries to pull the axe from the tree stump, but Yohei buried it so deep that Jiro cannot budge it. I see a smile of triumph playing on Yohei's face. But before Jiro can loosen the ax, the Emperor's Royal Game Warden steps into the clearing.

Yohei bows deeply. I try to read his face. Is he pleased? Worried? Is he afraid?

I can see that Jiro and Kane are shocked. They bow slightly, try to say something, but only sputter. I hear the Game Warden greet them with a samurai grunt. I hear Kane whisper to Jiro:

I thought you said
He never comes
This far north

                    Quiet woman
                    Jiro whispers back

Then he says:

                    Good Morning Sir
                    It is an honor to
                    Have you visit
                    Our humble farm
                    Jiro says
                    Is there something I
                    Can do for you
                              Sir

                    I am looking for the
                    Hunter who is
                    Shooting Royal Cranes
                    Have you seen him
                    Do you know who he
                              Is

                    The hunter who
                    Jiro says
                              Who, who
                    Yes well
                    I'll watch out for him, Sir
                    And if I find the
                              Culprit

Jiro and Kane begin to slink away, but Yohei yanks them back.

                    Sir
                    This poor farmer is sure
                    His esteemed landlord
                    Can help
                    He himself is
                    A hunter brave
                    Who fears nothing in the
                              Wild

The Game Warden grunts his approval and says to Jiro:

                    Then as a hunter brave
                    You know where to
                    Look for the poacher

Yes
Jiro says
But we must be going
          Sir

When the Game Warden is not looking, Jiro hides the broken arrow under his quilted coat. From behind my favorite tree, I want to shout:

Game Warden, look what he's hiding

But I know better. All he would hear would be the *kar-r-rooo* of a crane. I watch Jiro and Kane take another step to flee, but Yohei is too smart to let them get away. He says to the Game Warden:

Sir
Just this morning
Landlord Jiro took
The broken arrow
This ignorant farmer
Drew from the
Wounded crane

The same arrow
          Sir
That Thou found
In my poor hut

If a stupid farmer
Can be so bold
The arrow may lead
Thee to the
          Hunter

I am so proud of my sly, cunning husband that I tuck my beak under my healed wounded wing and laugh. The Game Warden grunts his approval, then says to Jiro:

Wait
Not so fast
          Fearless hunter

Sir
Jiro pleads

The arrow has no value
It is broken

Honored Sir
Yohei says
But look how
Beautiful it
          Is

The Game Warden grunts his approval and orders Jiro to give him the pieces of the broken arrow. He turns them over in his hands. Then he says:

This is an excellent arrow
Straight
Well crafted
As sharp as my
          Sword

Hunter, do you know
Whose arrow this is

No Sir
          Jiro says

I smile. The fool just talked his way into Yohei's trap. He says:

If this simple farmer
Can be so bold
He is certain
That the broken arrow
Does not belong to his
Esteemed
          Landlord

I am excited. I know what is going to happen next.

The Game Warden says
Is this your arrow
          Fearless Hunter

CHAPTER TWENTY-ONE
The Day is Now

Jiro says
I have never seen it before
      Today

Then why did you take it
From this poor farmer

Because
Kane says
Because this poor farmer is
A coward
Not a hunter brave
And

And I wanted the arrowhead
Jiro says
See how sharp it is and

And the farmer we own
Kane says
Has no use for it
He doesn't even have a
Bow

Keep your arrow then
The Game Warden says
Come
Help me catch the
Hunter who dares to
Harm or kill a
      Royal Crane

The Game Warden pats his samurai sword.

He will pay the
Terrible price

The Mighty Emperor has
Decreed

Jiro and Kane try to flee again, but Yohei tightens the leash.

Wise Sir
Hast thou noticed the
Feathers on the shaft

The Game Warden snatches the pieces of the broken arrow from
Jiro and eyes them closely.

White and black and red
Yohei says
Soft and silky

They look like, like
The Royal Game Warden says
Like
Not so fast
Hunter

Jiro and Kane freeze in their boot prints.

Ye-e-e-s
Jiro says
They look like
The feathers of a crane
But
But that is not my arrow

Yohei is a thief
Kane says
We ordered him
Off our land
He cheats
And

And refuses to pay
What he owes
Jiro says
Now he's just
Trying

Trying to get
Even
Kane says

Maybe
Yohei says
This ignorant farmer is wrong
He is sure the broken arrow
Does not match
The arrows in his Esteemed
                Landlord's
                Quiver

The Royal Game Warden yanks an arrow from the quiver. At the same time, he pushes Jiro to the ground and pins him with his boot. I quietly clap my wings in joy.

The roles are now reversed

It is a stupid landlord who now lies prone at the feet of a wise farmer. I whisper to Yohei, even though he cannot hear me:

As sure as
A crane sings *kar-r-ooo*
As winter weeps into spring
As carp splash in the Crystallake
Your day has
Come

I wait for the Game Warden to pronounce sentence in the name of the Mighty Emperor. I can already taste the sweetness of revenge. I am not ashamed to say that I cannot wait to see Jiro's head roll in the snow, red and ugly, eyes frozen wide in a forever fear.

The Game Warden stands as tall and straight as a spear. He says:

Hunter
Coward
You may fool this
Simple farmer
But you cannot fool me

Stupid husband
Kane says

But you wanted
A feather bed
Jiro says

But I didn't tell you
To shoot the Emperor's birdie
Kane says

Where else would I
Find feathers
On a squirrel

Wise sir
Kane purrs
Esteemed Royal Game Warden
          Of
The Mighty Emperor
This is not my arrow
I am just a-a-a
Weak woman who
Cannot pull the stiff string of a
          Bow

The Royal Game Warden ties Jiro's hands with a leather thong.
Then, he stands as tall as a spear and says:

The Mighty Emperor has decreed
That no man has the right
To hunt a Royal Crane
To shoot it day or night

Please sir
Kane pleads
I am just a wife who cooks
What her husband kills

Woman
The Game Warden says
The Emperor is as fair as
He is just

In his name I decree
You are free to
          Go

111

Then the Game Warden says to Jiro who is quivering like a
snowbunnie:

> As for you
> Conniving coward
> The Just Emperor has decreed
>
> Death shall befall
> The man who dares to
> Harm or kill
> What brings joy to all
>
> But wise Sir
> Jiro pleads
> It was just a bird
>
> Just a birdie Sir
> Kane pleads
> What will happen to me
>
> Who cares
> The Game Warden says
>
> But
> Where will I live
>
> In a cave
> Under a rock
> Up a tree
> The Game Warden says
>
> But
> What will I do
>
> Cut wood
> The Game Warden says
>
> But
> My hands are as
> Soft as my kimono
> Kane whines
> It's
> It's
>   Not Fair

Fair is for the rich
The Game Warden says
All the poor get is
        More Work

CHAPTER TWENTY-TWO

A Heart of Gold

The Game Warden asks Yohei to kneel. He places his sword on
Yohei's shoulder and says:

> Brave farmer
> In the name of the
> Mighty Emperor
> I give you
> This hut
> > All
> The fields you farm
> > All
> The trees you harvest
>
> I give you the title
> > SIR
>
> I give you
> The hunter's mansion
> > On
> The Crystallake
> > All
> The things in it
>
> I give you
> His horses
> His bows
> His arrows
> His jeweled
> > Sword
>
> Just sir
> Yohei says
> I do not deserve
> Such kindness
> Such honor
> All I want are the fields

I farm
The trees
I harvest
My humble hut
Filled
With memories of love
And
Pains of loss

I would be grateful
Sir
If you divided the
Rest
Among the poor
Farmers

The Game Warden grunts his approval. I am stunned and proud that Yohei would give up riches to help others. And I am moved to cranetears that he chooses to stay in his hut, our home, to caress the memories of his beautiful Tsuu.

The Game Warden raises his sword over Jiro, whose face is as white as my feathers. Kane turns her back, unable to watch her husband's head stain the snow red.

As for me, the moment I have been waiting for has finally come. Justice for Yohei. Revenge for me. There is no mercy in the moral code of cranes. Just unforgiving justice and

No Second Chance

I study Yohei's face to see if he is as pleased as I am. I wonder what he is thinking. But not for long.

My husband bows to the Game Warden and says:

Sir
Can I keep the
Broken arrow

It is all I have to
Remind me of a love
Lost

The Game Warden lowers his sword and gives Yohei the broken arrow that binds me to him. Then he raises his word over Jiro's naked neck. But before he can strike the mighty blow, Yohei shocks me again. He says:

Sir
You are as just as
You are wise

If the Mighty Emperor wants to
Punish Jiro for
Hunting Royal Cranes
Let him live

Without money
Without land
Without title
He will pay for his crime
Forever

The Game Warden grunts his approval and lowers his sword. He says:

Because you caught this
Worthless coward
It is yours to seal his fate
So
As Game Warden of the
Mighty Emperor
I decree

He will live as a
Poor farmer
For the rest of his mortal
Life

The Game Warden sheathes his samurai sword and unties Jiro's hands. Jiro and Kane bound into the pine forest like white-tailed deer. Then the Game Warden rests his hand on Yohei's bowed head, nods his approval and vanishes into the snowy pines.

Yohei scans the sky in a desperate hope see me. To share this moment of justice. Then he kisses the broken arrow, as if it were me. Then he kneels and buries it in the spot in the clearing where he goes every morning to scatter wild rice. Then he bows his head low like a beggar outside the Emperor's Palace. He says:

I know you cannot forgive me
My Tsuu
I failed to keep my
Sacred promise

I know I have no right to ask
          But
When the snow
Drifts against pine trunks
          And
Turns the needles white
Come back
My beautiful Tsuu
Yohei will be waiting
Still paying the price
          Of
          Betrayal

When you looked at me
Eyes twinkling bright
The room took on a glow
But I did not hold you tight
I made you
          Go

    I argue with myself as I listen to Yohei rip open his heart. Mortal men make mistakes. Should I not forgive?

When you laughed with me
Eyes burning bright
My cares melted like
          Morning Frost

I held a moonbeam in my hand
A lovely song in my heart
But I didn't hold you tight
I made you
          Go

    My weeping heart asks: How can you *not* forgive him?

What have you done
          Fool
You drove her away
No one to blame but you
Foolish, foolish, foolish
          Man

    I listen to my heart. I whisper through my tears:

I forgive you
My husband

I Love You So

CHAPTER TWENTY-THREE

The Choice

Once again, I hide behind my favorite tree and wait for the night to drop its black curtain. For the forest to breathe softly. For my husband to find sleep. Then I creep up to the hut and peek through the window. The embers in the firepit wink at me. I quietly open the door and tiptoe inside.

My long black hair is laced with three ribbons. Red, black, and white. My tiny feet are silent on the earthen floor. I kneel by my husband's side. My heart has spoken clearly and I have listened. I know what I must do. I cannot breathe. What if he is too frightened to listen to *his* heart?

I say softly so as not to wake him:

> Sleep
> My husband
> Sleep
>
> Rest your weary head
> May the stars above
> Send you sweet peace
>
> When you awake
> I will be here
> For my love is forever
> And yours to keep
> Sleep
> My husband
> Sleep

Then I lean over and kiss his brow.

> I have given you
> All I have left to
> Give
>
> Choose wisely
> My husband

> I will await your
> Answer
>
> Whatever you choose
> I am your Tsuu
> Your wife
>> Forever

I tiptoe out of the hut just before the sun paints the sky. I wait for my husband to wake. I am so nervous that I pace around the pines on my long legs, as thin as hickory sticks, until I am too tired to walk.

I stop and watch for the golden fingers of dawn to end their creep across the darkness. Then I walk to the far edge of the clearing and stand where my husband can see me. Tall and straight as a crane can be, I face the hut and I pray.

The door flies open. My husband rushes out. He looks so handsome with his long, graceful neck. Red, black, and white feathers. Legs as strong as hickory sticks.

I rush toward him. I reach the middle of the clearing. I am so dizzy with happiness that I stumble. My husband catches me. He flaps his mighty wings in greeting. He dances around me like a joyous chick.

We fly up, up into the goldsky. Wing to wing, we fly. Higher and higher. As free as we can be.

> Just joy
> Our love
> And we

THE BEGINNING

Afterlog

I am the Royal Game Warden
By this time
You know me well
I played an important role
In the beautiful love story of
Tsuu and Yohei

I am sure you
Would like to know what
Happened to them
So let me tell you

Each winter's week
I stand amid the
Snow-crusted pines near
Yohei's empty hut
I hold
A leather bag
Filled with wild rice

And each time
Two cranes
White and black and red
Come to eat from my hand

I close my eyes
And I listen and
I hear a woman sing
And you can too
If you listen with
Your heart

We are as free as light
And all that we can be
Our love is forever
   Just joy
Our wings and

   We

127

www.ingramcontent.com/pod-product-compliance
Lightning Source LLC
Chambersburg PA
CBHW051120300726
48981CB00002B/198